Seven o'clock in the morning.

Someone is resting
by the lotus pond.

Someone is cycling
through the park.

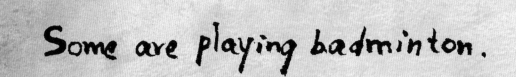

Some are playing badminton.

Lots of people are waltzing.

Others are exercising.

Some are doing tai chi.

Others like sword dancing.

A couple are pushing hands.

Friends play chess.

An artist draws.

Three are stretching.

A group throws a shuttlecock.

Others like to play cards.

People dance with fans.